Stories and Poems

LITTLE Lit+

Book 3

Santillana
Spotlight
on English

Stories and Rhymes

Little Book 3

Rebecca Williams Salvador

THE ENORMOUS CARROT

A father planted a carrot seed. It
grew and it grew. The father pulled
the carrot, but it didn't come out.

The father called to the mother, "Help me
pull out this carrot, please." They pulled and
they pulled, but it didn't come out.

The mother called to the brother,
"Help us pull out this carrot."
They pulled and they pulled, but
it didn't come out.

Along came the baby sister. The baby pulled on the brother, the brother pulled on the mother, the mother pulled on the father. The carrot finally came out! The mother made carrot soup for everyone.

Rub-a-dub-dub,
Three men in a tub.
And who do you think they be?

The butcher, the baker,
The candlestick maker,
And all of them gone to sea.

Watch it Grow

Here's a little seed.
Plant it in the ground.

Water it, water it, water all around.

Add a little sunshine. Just like so.

Watch the plant, watch
the plant, watch it grow.

I'm Going to the Beach Today

Hip, hip hurray!
I'm on my way!
I'm going to the beach today.

I have my shovel,
My bucket, too.
I'm ready to go.
How about you?

We can build a castle.
We can swim and play.
We can have some fun at the beach today.

We'll splash about.
We'll sit in the sun.
Let's go to the beach and have some fun.

17

The eentsy weentsy spider,
Went up the waterspout.

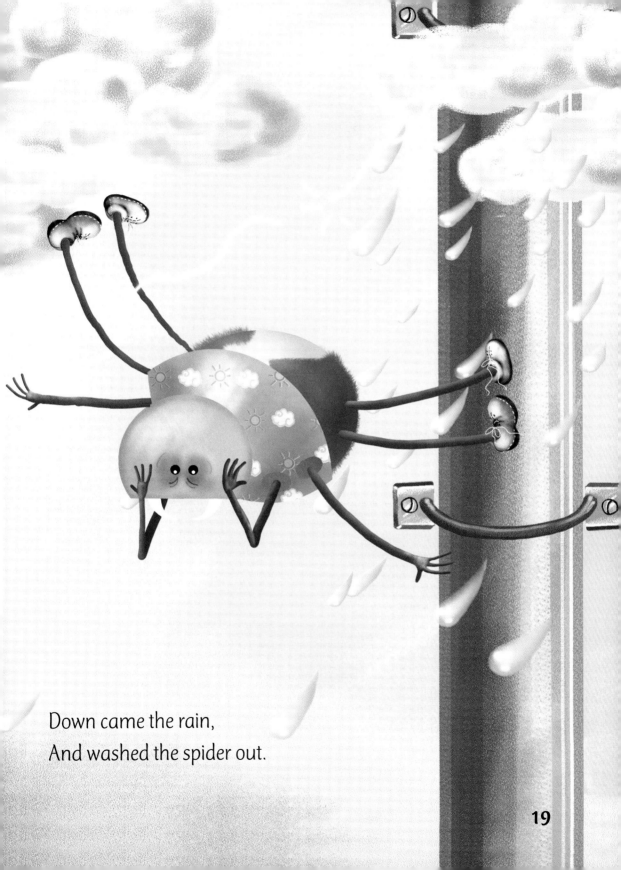

Down came the rain,
And washed the spider out.

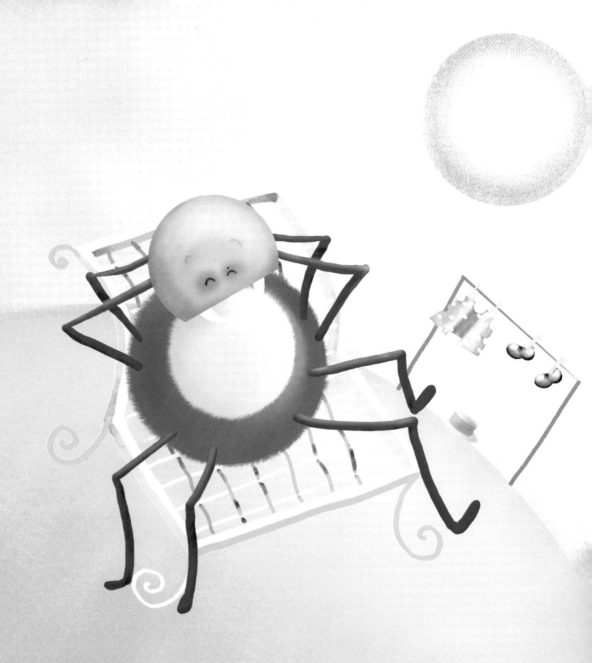

Out came the sun,
And dried up all the rain.

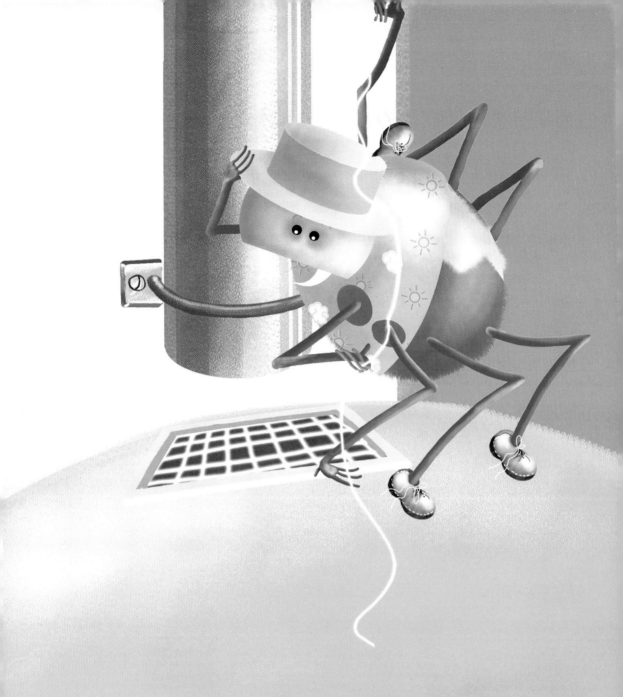

And the eentsy weentsy spider,
Went up the spout again.

Stories and Rhymes 3 includes selections from
Sprinkles 1, Sprinkles 2, and Sprinkles 3 published by
RICHMOND PUBLISHING
Av. Universidad 767
Col. Del Valle
03100 México, D.F.

Publisher: *Alicia Becker*
Development Editor: *Lauren Robbins*
Editor: *Anita Heald*
Proofreaders: *Jorge Mancera, Justine Piekarowicz, Mary Todd, Dominic Wright,
Richard Godnick, Lawrence Lipson*

Design Supervisor: *Marisela Pérez*
Design: *Isabel Arnaud*
Cover Design: *Isabel Arnaud*
Cover Illustration: *Dalia Alvarado, Isabel Arnaud, Gabriel Pacheco*
Art Direction: *Isabel Arnaud*
Layout and DTP: *Marilú Jiménez, Susana Rojas*

Illustrations: *Dalia Alvarado, Isabel Arnaud, Gabriel Pacheco*

Technical Coordination: *Salvador Pereira*
Technical Assistance: *José Luis Avila, Daniel Santillán*

© 2003 by Editorial Santillana, S.A. de C.V.

This edition:

© 2008 Santillana USA Publishing Company, Inc.
2105 NW 86th Avenue
Miami, FL 33122

Published in the United States of America.
Santillana Spotlight on English Thematic Library Level K
Stories and Rhymes 3 Little Book
ISBN 10: 1-59820-556-0
ISBN 13: 978-1-59820-556-5
Printed in Colombia by Quebecor World Bogotá S.A.
12 11 10 09 08   1 2 3 4 5 6 7 8 9 10